WELCOM

Collect the special coins in this book.
You will earn one gold coin for
every chapter you read.

Once you have finished all the chapters,
find out what to do with your gold coins at
the back of the book.

With special thanks to Tabitha Jones

For Oliver and Rufus Swann,
in loving memory of Klim Forster

www.beastquest.co.uk

ORCHARD BOOKS

First published in Great Britain in 2018 by The Watts Publishing Group

1 3 5 7 9 10 8 6 4 2

Text © 2018 Beast Quest Limited.
Cover and inside illustrations by Steve Sims
© Beast Quest Limited 2018

Beast Quest is a registered trademark of Beast Quest Limited
Series created by Beast Quest Limited, London

A CIP catalogue record for this book is available from the British Library.

ISBN 978 1 40834 305 0

Printed in Great Britain

The paper and board used in this book are made from wood from responsible sources

Orchard Books
An imprint of Hachette Children's Group
Part of The Watts Publishing Group Limited
Carmelite House, 50 Victoria Embankment, London EC4Y 0DZ

An Hachette UK Company
www.hachette.co.uk
www.hachettechildrens.co.uk

OSPIRA
THE SAVAGE SORCERESS

BY ADAM BLADE

ORCHARD

CONTENTS

STORY ONE

DARK SECRETS

By the light of a single candle I pack what I need. An extra cloak for the journey; some bread and cheese to sustain me. This may be a one-way trip.

I once took an oath, to serve my king without question. To treat him honestly, always.

To my shame, I broke that oath some years ago. My loyalty torn, I chose to lie.

And now the past that I thought was buried in darkness has found its way into the light. I blow out the candle, and its trail of grey smoke twists away.

I must leave the palace, under cover of night. If I never see these walls again – if this journey is the end of me – so be it. It is little more than I deserve...

Aduro,
former wizard to King Hugo

RETURNING HOME

"I can't wait to get back and see Uncle Henry and Aunt Maria," Tom said, turning to Elenna as they headed down the corridor. Tapestries of ancient battles hung from the walls, showing armies of knights in armour clashing with one another. "It seems a long time since I last made it home."

Elenna raised an eyebrow, grinning. "Maybe we actually will make it there this time without something terrible—Whoa!" Daltec barrelled out of a side passage, almost ploughing into them. He stepped back, looking pale.

"Are you all right?" Elenna asked.

"I'm searching for Aduro," Daltec said breathlessly. "I can't find him anywhere and I've checked his chambers, the library, the Gallery of Tombs…"

"Maybe he's in the garden gathering herbs," Elenna said. "It's just the weather for it."

Daltec's expression brightened. "Good thinking!" he said, then turned and dashed away. Tom and Elenna exchanged puzzled shrugs then continued towards the throne room.

As they neared the door, Tom heard fierce, throaty growls coming from inside. Adrenaline fizzed through his veins. He froze, his hand on the hilt of his sword. *A Beast in the palace!* Elenna shot Tom a worried glance and tugged her bow from her back as the growling rose to a hideous, slavering snarl. They charged through the door, weapons raised...

...only to find King Hugo bent over

Prince Thomas's crib, his hands curled into claws. A high-pitched giggle erupted from the cot. Tom and Elenna tucked their weapons away, grinning with relief. Queen Aroha, seated on her throne beside the cot, covered her mouth with a hand, trying to smother a laugh.

The king straightened, blushing fiercely. "Er… Hello, Tom…Elenna. I'm glad to see you are always ready to defend your prince." He brushed down his robes and took his seat beside Aroha. She wiped away a tear, still chuckling.

"And I'm glad you arrived when you did," Aroha said. "Thomas has been giggling so hard I feared he might lose his lunch. Would you like to hold him?"

Tom heard a squelchy hiccup from the baby's cot and put up his hands, "Er... No, thank you. We actually came to ask if we could take a few days' leave to visit Errinel."

King Hugo frowned gravely, shaking his head, and Tom's spirits sank. *What is it now? A Beast...or maybe pirates?*

"I can only spare you on one condition," the king said, and Tom noticed a twinkle in his eye. "You must bring back a piece of your aunt's cherry pie for Queen Aroha. She insists that Tangalan cuisine is far superior to Avantian – but I'm confident one bite of Maria's speciality will change her mind."

Tom grinned. "Of course," he said.

"I'll do better than that. I'll—" A grizzly cry erupted from the prince's crib, drowning out Tom's words.

"Hush, hush," Aroha said, rocking the cot, but the grizzles quickly escalated to full-blown wails.

"Time someone went down for a nap, I think," Aroha said. "Ursula!" At the queen's call, an embroidered curtain on the far side of the room rustled. A small, plumpish woman with glinting eyes and rosy cheeks stepped from behind it. Silver hair curled from around the edge of her dark headscarf, and she wore a neat black dress and a white apron. She smiled as she gazed down into the prince's cot, then bent to lift him in her arms. As soon as Thomas's head rested against the woman's shoulder, his cries softened, then fell silent. He let out a delighted giggle, and grabbed at a roughly carved red stone hanging from a gold chain about her throat. Ursula laughed and gently

unfastened the prince's pudgy fingers.

"It wouldn't do for you to cut your little handsies now, would it?" she said. "Have this instead." Ursula pulled a small, button-eyed rabbit from her pocket and pressed it into the prince's hand. The prince shoved the toy's ear into his mouth.

"Ursula has such a way with babies," King Hugo said. "Ursula, please meet Tom, our Master of Beasts, and his companion, Elenna."

"I have heard so much about you," Ursula said, fixing Tom with keen grey eyes. Tom shifted uncomfortably, suddenly uneasy under the woman's gaze. "May I say, you are the very image of your father," she went on.

"You knew Taladon?" Tom asked

Ursula, surprised.

"I wouldn't say I *knew* him," Ursula said. "He visited my hometown in Rion when he was not that much older than you are now. Everyone thought he was so *very* dashing." Tom looked sharply at Ursula, thinking her tone sounded slightly mocking. But she smiled back at him, her eyes clear and bright.

"You're from Rion?" Elenna asked. "I wouldn't have guessed from your accent. You hardly have one at all."

Ursula stiffened, and a flicker of a frown crossed her face. But then she blinked, and her warm smile returned. Now it was coupled with a sad, wistful look in her eyes. "No? Well, as a nanny I have lived most of my life away from home."

Ursula lifted Prince Thomas from her shoulder and chuckled merrily, wrinkling her nose as she gazed into his round face. "I think you might need a change!" she said. Then she turned to the queen and king and bobbed a half curtsy. "If you will excuse me, I'll take our little prince up to get ready for his nap now." Aroha nodded, and Ursula left them, her long skirt swishing as it brushed the flagstones behind her.

"Well, I suppose we had better take our leave too," Tom said, bowing to first the king, then the queen. "After all, we have been charged with a very important Quest – to fetch a cherry pie! Elenna, let's collect our things, and I'll meet you at the stables."

As Tom crossed the courtyard, the morning air felt crisp and fresh, but bright sunlight warmed his skin. *Perfect weather for riding*, he thought. *I can't wait to get back home!* Something red glinted in the corner of his eye. Tom glanced up towards it, then stopped to look closer. A window on the third floor of the west tower glowed red. *Fire?* But the light seemed too steady, and too deep a colour. Tom called on the enhanced eyesight of his golden helmet, just one of the powers granted to him by the magical suit of armour stored safely in the palace armoury. Gazing through the window with sharpened vision, he could see

Ursula holding baby Thomas out at arm's length. But something was wrong and Tom's stomach squirmed. A scarlet smoke poured from her open mouth and snaked around the baby. The hideous, red-tinged tableau

filled Tom with horror. *Witchcraft!* He spun, his heart pounding, and dashed back into the courtyard to find Daltec striding towards him.

"Tom! I still haven't found Aduro!" Daltec said, wringing his hands.

"Baby Thomas is in danger!" Tom cried. "We can look for Aduro later. Come with me!" Tom raced away without waiting for an answer. He sped across the courtyard and crashed through the main palace doors and into the throne room.

"Tom! Quiet, or you'll wake Thomas!" Queen Aroha cried.

"The baby is in terrible danger," Tom told her, then raced on.

Aroha gasped. "What do you mean?" But Tom couldn't lose time explaining. Aroha and Hugo's footsteps joined Daltec's behind him as he sprinted from the room, darting along corridors and finally clattering up the west tower's spiral stair.

As Tom threw open the nursery door, his heart leapt with horror. The room was empty.

Baby Thomas, and his nanny too, were gone.

2

KIDNAP

Queen Aroha let out a wail of
anguish. "Ursula!" she cried. "Where
are you?! Where's my baby?"

"They must be nearby," Hugo said,
glancing about. "Ursula can't have
left. The guards wouldn't let anyone
take Thomas from the palace without
our permission. And why would she
take him, anyway?"

Tom scanned the vacant chamber.

The curtains fluttered in a breeze from the open window. He crossed the room, his stomach knotting with worry. Peering out, he spied Elenna, heading towards the stables. And, hanging from grappling hooks attached to the window ledge outside, a long rope

ladder reached all the way to the ground. *But how could an old lady have the strength to make such a climb?*

"Elenna!" Tom called out. She looked up from below. "Ursula has kidnapped the prince. Go and tell Captain Harkman to lock the city gates. No one must leave until we find him." Elenna's eyes widened with shock, then she nodded and set off at a run.

"My baby… Why would she take him?" Aroha breathed, pale and hunched over as if she'd been punched in the stomach. "She was so good with him. She seemed like the perfect nanny."

"I can't believe it of her!" Hugo said,

shaking his head. "It makes no sense!"

"First Aduro. Now Thomas and Ursula," Daltec muttered. "What's going on?"

"While there's blood in my veins, I mean to find out!" Tom growled. He strode from the room, followed closely by the king, queen and Daltec. They reached the throne room just as Elenna entered with Captain Harkman.

"Your Majesties!" Harkman said, dropping to one knee, his face lined with remorse. "Ursula left the palace on a mule. She said she was going to watch the royal falcons fly outside the city walls. If only I had thought to check the basket she had with her—"

"She cannot have gone far!" Queen

Aroha said, her eyes flashing. "Send your swiftest men at once. Bring my son home!"

Tom and Elenna were already halfway to the door.

They raced to the stables, where Tom saddled Storm. Putting his hand on Tagus's horseshoe, embedded in his shield, Tom called on its magical speed, then leapt on to his horse's back. Elenna swung up behind him, and they galloped from the palace grounds.

With the city walls behind them, Tom slowed his steed and called on the enhanced sight of his golden helmet. Ahead, he could see a merchant's cart throwing up clouds of dust, and further along the road, a farmer driving a herd of cows. Then finally, on a narrow dirt track crossing a field, he spotted a lone mule carrying a small figure in a dark cloak. *Ursula!*

Tom urged Storm back to full speed. Fields, green with budding crops, passed by in a blur on either side as Storm thundered onwards. They left the City far behind, finally nearing the mossy banks of a river.

"There!" Elenna cried, pointing. Relief flooded Tom's chest as he saw Ursula sitting cross-legged on the sunny riverbank with Prince Thomas cradled in one arm, asleep. But Tom's relief quickly changed to alarm. In her other hand, Ursula held the red stone pendant she had worn about her neck, turning it slowly so that its sharp edges and facets glinted in the sun. As Storm raced closer, Ursula glanced up at Tom and Elenna, smiling, then ran her thumb along the amulet to its knife-like point.

Tom tugged Storm to a halt and

swung down from the saddle. "Give me the baby, now!" he cried. Elenna leapt down behind him, her bow ready in her hands. Ursula fixed Tom with her glinting grey eyes, then smiled fondly down at the prince, holding her sharp-edged stone dangerously close to the baby's throat.

"I don't think I shall," Ursula said, still gazing at the sleeping baby. "I'll be a far better mother to my little prince than anyone else could be." Then she started to sing in a high, sweet voice – a haunting melody that seemed to loop and swirl in Tom's mind like the swooping flight of a bird. Tom staggered, suddenly dizzy. His limbs felt heavy and his eyelids drooped. A strange red mist poured from Ursula's mouth, mingling somehow with the song in Tom's head, curling and drifting through his muddled thoughts…through the shadows, then finally through darkness.

Tom's head throbbed with a dull ache and his tongue felt swollen and dry. He opened his eyes a slit, then closed them again, wincing in pain as yellow candlelight seared through his brain like fire. *What's happened? Am I still on a Quest?* He forced his eyes open once more, and tried to sit up, but firm hands pushed him back on to soft pillows.

"Rest," came Harkman's voice from beside him. Beyond the captain, Tom recognised the stone walls and high windows of the palace infirmary. And suddenly memories flooded his mind. The riverbank…Ursula…the red mist. *Baby Thomas!* He sat bolt upright

and scanned the room. Elenna lay
in the bed beside Tom's, her eyelids
flickering as she began to stir. Queen
Aroha stood nearby with King Hugo.

"What happened?" Tom asked.

"Yes…" Elenna said, rubbing her
eyes. "How did we get here?"

"We found you unconscious beside
the river," Captain Harkman said.
"Even Storm was asleep. My men
brought you back to the palace. I
went on, in pursuit of Ursula and the
prince…" The captain's voice faltered,
and he lowered his eyes, shaking his
head. "I found no sign. It is as if they
vanished."

"They have to be somewhere!"
Aroha growled, her voice ragged with
anger and grief.

"I'm sorry, Aroha," Tom said, hardly able to look at her drawn face. "We failed you."

Aroha shook her head. "No!" She almost spat the word. "I failed my baby! I should never have trusted that woman!"

King Hugo took the queen's hand in his own. "Ursula took us all by surprise," he said. Aroha closed her eyes, her jaw clenched with anguish.

Tom leapt from his bed and bowed low before her. "Your Majesty," he said, "I shan't fail you twice. Elenna and I will head back out at once. We won't rest until Prince Thomas is found."

A sudden commotion at the door made everyone turn. Daltec burst into the room, his face haggard and grey.

"Have you found Aduro?" Elenna
asked.

"No," Daltec said gravely. He held
out a leatherbound book in a shaking
hand, the pages open. "But I found

this in his quarters. It's a journal."

Tom came closer and cast his eyes over the looping script. "That's not Aduro's writing," he said.

"No…" Daltec's voice faltered, and he swallowed hard. "No. This belongs to his sister."

Tom gasped. "His sister? In all the time I've known Aduro, he never once mentioned a sister!" *Which makes me wonder what else he's been hiding…*

King Hugo frowned, his eyes suddenly sad and troubled. "Ospira was her name," he said quietly, "but she died long ago."

"Perhaps not," said Daltec, and fear played over his features.

"What in all Avantia do you mean?" asked King Hugo.

Daltec was trembling. "Sire, I think the simplest way to explain might be to read to you."

"We don't have time for this!" said Aroha.

Hugo put an arm around his wife. "My queen, hear the boy out. I want to find our son as much as you, but I fear we are dealing with something more complicated than a kidnapping." He turned to Daltec. "Read quickly. We are listening."

Daltec opened the book, and – slowly, at first – he began to read.

OSPIRA'S JOURNAL:
THE BEGINNING

Taladon – or "The Hero", as everyone insists on calling him – came back to the palace today after yet another pointless Quest, fighting some Beast or other.

As always, everyone made a great fuss, but frankly, I'm not impressed. All the stories sound the same to me – Taladon the Brilliant rides off on

his mighty steed to face some poor creature or other with claws, or fangs, or poison spines. All seems lost! The creature is unbeatable! Until, ta dah! What a surprise, the hero triumphs... again.

I can still hear the men going on about it now, celebrating in the throne room. Hugo and my brother can't seem to get enough of Taladon's endless bragging. It's quite pathetic, really.

But at least it keeps them out of my way while I get on with more important things. I managed to copy several very interesting spells from my darling brother's magic books while they were all busy congratulating each other on how amazing they all are.

Of course, I would rather not have to sneak about behind Aduro's back, but he has left me no choice. A few weeks ago, he walked in on me while I was practising levitation – a basic spell even a child could master, but he became quite wild! He said I had no idea what I was doing, and that I'd get myself in trouble. Which is hardly fair, considering I keep asking him to teach me properly – but of course he always says no. Magic isn't a toy, blah blah blah. He even had the nerve to call me untrustworthy! Frankly, I think he's afraid. He knows I'd quickly become more powerful than he is. He just wants to keep all the magic for himself. Typical!

And now I'm sure he's got that pimpled clown of a pageboy spying on me – Hardman or Herman or whatever his name is. I can barely turn around without tripping over his oversized feet. But I managed to sneak past him while he was polishing his boots and went to listen in on one of my brother and Taladon's secret chats.

And this is the exciting bit of news I've been saving. They were talking about an artefact Taladon found on his Quest to the Stonewin Volcano. I got a look at it through the keyhole – a tooth-shaped piece of red volcanic glass. I could tell Aduro knew what it was at once – his face turned white, like a child afraid of the dark. He told Taladon the thing was one of the sorcerer Derthsin's possessions – a magical talisman that would have been better left where it was.

Of course, that just made it sound all the more interesting. So I took myself off to the library, and, after several hours' reading, I found it! There was a picture of the exact same stone in one of the Chronicles of Avantia, *drawn by a long-dead wizard called Rufus. He found it while searching among Derthsin's possessions, and thought it safer to leave it in the volcano. Coward!*

I put a sleeping spell on the nosy librarian, so I could take the book to my room. Now I have it here, right in front of me. And I can tell you, after reading about what that amulet can do, my heart is thumping! It won't be easy, given the way Aduro guards his possessions, but I absolutely must have it!

4

MOUNTAIN AMBUSH

"Wait!" Tom said, interrupting Daltec's reading. "I've seen that amulet! Ursula wears it about her neck! Do you think she could really be Aduro's sister?"

Elenna frowned thoughtfully. "She'd be about the right age. And she's got those piercing grey eyes, very like Aduro's."

Harkman nodded his head slowly. "Come to think of it, I did think she looked strangely familiar. It was a long time ago I last saw Ospira, and I was very young...but it could be her."

Hugo frowned. "Maybe there is a slight likeness. But Ospira died. Or at least that's what Aduro said." Hugo paused, gnawing his lip. "Although... she was a long way from home when she became ill, and her body was never returned to Avantia."

"Hmm. And now Aduro's missing too," Elenna said. "That can't just be a coincidence. And it sounds like it's all got something to do with that stone. Daltec – do we even know what the talisman does?"

Daltec took a shaky breath. "Not

precisely," he said. "However, I have my suspicions. When Derthsin died, he was trying to find new ways to create Beasts that he could control."

A sudden memory of the way Ursula had looked at the red stone while cradling baby Thomas made Tom shudder. *What hideous thing might she to do to the prince?*

"We can't waste any more time talking!" Aroha snapped. From the horror in her eyes, Tom guessed that she'd been thinking the same thing. "Daltec – you have to use your magic to track down Aduro. He must know something about what's going on!"

Daltec swallowed, then nodded. He drew a small, blue-tinted crystal ball from his pocket, and cupped

it in the palm of his hand. Tom and
Elenna, along with the king, the queen
and Captain Harkman, crowded close
while Daltec passed his free hand over
the crystal ball and muttered a few
magical words.

The crystal ball seemed to mist over

with swirling clouds of white. *Snow!*
Tom realised. And, looking more
closely, he could see a cloaked form
with a long beard and a staff, bent
double against the wind. *Aduro!* The
old man toiled across a rocky plain.
Through the snow, Tom could just
make out the shadowy forms of the
Northern Mountains in the distance.

"What is he doing?" King Hugo
asked. "He'll never survive such a
journey!"

"Can you bring him back?" Aroha
asked.

"I'll try," Daltec said. He frowned
down at the image in the crystal.
Before long, his hand began to shake.
Sweat beaded his brow. He let out a
gasp, then lifted his eyes. "I can't even

speak with him. Some sort of magical interference is blocking my powers."

"What does that mean?" Aroha asked.

"Arcta might know," Tom said. "Not much happens in the north that he isn't aware of." Tom put one hand to the red jewel in his belt and rested the other on the magical feather Arcta had given him, now embedded in his shield. *Arcta,* Tom called, reaching out to the mountain giant with his mind. Nothing. Tom tried again, but it felt as if an invisible wall shielded the Good Beast from his efforts. Dread twisted in his gut. "I can't reach him," Tom said. "Elenna's right. This must all be connected somehow – Aduro, Ospira, the red stone, and now this strange magic in the north."

"I agree," Queen Aroha said. "Tom and Elenna, go after Aduro at once. Find out everything he knows about his sister and where she might be taking my child." Aroha turned to Captain Harkman. "Captain, send out your best men. Scour the whole of Avantia. No one returns until that woman is found, and my son is home where he belongs."

Without waiting for dawn, Tom and Elenna threw on winter cloaks and rode out together on Storm. As they passed from the high city gates on to the open road, Tom heard the wild clatter of hoofbeats behind them. He glanced back to see Queen Aroha riding her chestnut horse, Hurricane,

her cloak billowing in the wind.

Tom slowed Storm to a trot.

"This trip is too dangerous," he told Aroha as she drew up alongside. "The people need you. You should return to the palace. We'll find Aduro and bring Thomas home, I promise."

The queen gazed back at him, her eyes bright and fierce. "I don't need your advice," she said. Then she tapped her heels to her Tangalan stallion's sides and shot ahead. "Keep up if you can," she called back.

Tom hands felt numb with cold as he tugged on the reins, pulling Storm to a halt. They had ridden hard for a full day and night, leaving the green shoots and delicate blossoms of spring far behind them. Now a pale sun rose over the peaks of the Northern Mountains ahead, making the dusting of snow on the rocky ground glitter.

Queen Aroha drew up beside Storm.

"Why are we stopping?" she asked.

"I'm going to try and contact Arcta again, now we're close to his home," Tom said. He put his hand once more to the red jewel in his belt, and touched the eagle feather in his shield. *Arcta*, he called. *Can you hear me?* This time the red stone glowed hot, and a sudden rush of emotion took Tom's breath away – fear, pain and fury. But still the Beast didn't answer. Tom gritted his teeth. "Arcta heard me," Tom told the others. "But something is wrong. I think we must be nearing the source of whatever strange power is at work here."

They rode onwards between high, craggy outcrops of rock, searching the barren landscape for any sign of

Aduro or his sister. The hollow ring of their horses' hooves echoed in the icy air. As they neared the mountains, boulders and rubble from landslides littered the ground. Stunted thorn bushes clung to the rock, twisted into strange, tortured shapes by the relentless wind. Suddenly Elenna gasped, pointing at a clump of ragged briar. A scrap of deep blue cloth hung on the thorns, flapping in the breeze. Tom pulled his stallion to a halt and looked more closely at the tattered fabric. He made out a golden star...a sliver of a moon. His chest tightened with worry.

"Part of Aduro's cloak," Tom said.

"Look out!" Aroha shouted, her horse's hooves clattering on rock as she spurred him away. Tom looked up to see a huge boulder speeding towards them though the air. His heart leapt. He yanked Storm's reins and the stallion wheeled out of range, his front hooves striking sparks from the ground. *CRASH!* Tom felt the impact judder up through his horse's body as the giant rock crushed the thorn bush he'd been studying.

Another rock followed close behind the first. Tom and Aroha steered their horses away, but more boulders followed, arcing down from the mountain above in a deadly barrage.

"Up there!" Elenna cried, clutching at Tom's arm. Tom glanced up the mountainside to see a huge, hairy form step from behind a jagged

outcrop on to a narrow ridge. *Arcta!*
The Good Beast held another vast
boulder between his hands, and as
Tom watched, his heart in his throat,
Arcta lifted it high. "He's attacking
us!" Elenna exclaimed.

A BEAST ENSNARED

Tom leapt from Storm's back and drew his blade. Elenna swung down behind him, her bow ready, and Aroha joined them, brandishing her sword as Storm and Hurricane clattered away across the rocky plain.

"ROOOAAAR!" Arcta boomed from his ledge, making the whole mountain quake.

"I thought he was supposed to be a

friendly Beast," Aroha hissed.

Before Tom could answer, Arcta sent his boulder flying towards them.

"Run!" Tom cried. He leapt aside as Elenna and Aroha dived out of the missile's path. The rock landed with a *CRASH* that almost threw Tom off his feet. He caught his balance and stood his ground, lifting his eyes to those of the Beast. Arcta stared back at him, gnashing his teeth with fury. Tom took a step closer to the mountain giant, then another, his hand on the red jewel in his belt.

"Arcta! Stop! It's me, Tom!" he called. But the Beast roared, shaking his massive, shaggy head from side to side, his single eye bloodshot and wild.

"ROOOAAAR!" Arcta bent to pick

up another boulder.

"He's under some sort of enchantment," Tom called to Elenna and Aroha. "We need to split up. You two, keep him busy! I'll go in from above."

Elenna dived behind a fallen boulder and fired an arrow towards the Beast. It pinged off the ground at his feet, making him leap back with a growl. Tom set off at a crouching run, skirting from rock to rock, heading for higher ground as Arcta bent to lift another missile. *CRASH!* Arcta's rock slammed into the boulder that sheltered Elenna, smashing it, but she was already running in the other direction.

"Over here!" Tom heard Aroha cry.

He glanced back to see the queen standing straight and proud, her gleaming sword raised. "Fight me fair, you lumbering Beast!" she called.

Arcta's red eye seemed to bulge with rage as it swivelled towards the queen. He leapt down from his ledge with a boom that sent loose scree skittering down the mountain, then lurched towards Aroha. Another of Elenna's arrows whizzed through the air, striking the rocky ground in Arcta's path. The Beast raised his fists and shook them in fury, then continued towards the queen. Tom vaulted down on to the debris-strewn ledge where Arcta had stood.

Below him, the Beast closed in on Aroha, each of his ragged breaths a

harsh, menacing growl.

Tom selected the largest rock he could find, then, using the magical strength of the golden breastplate, he hefted it above his head. *Sorry, old friend!* he thought, and with a grunt he sent the missile flying. Arcta made a swipe for Aroha with a shaggy fist, but before the blow could land, the rock struck him on the back of the head. The Beast lifted a hand to his temple, swayed gently, then toppled backwards, landing at Aroha's feet with a mighty crash.

Aroha dropped to her knees at the Beast's side. Tom and Elenna ran to join her. Tom felt a wave of pity as he took in Arcta's slack, hollow-eyed face, lined with fatigue. Whatever spell controlled the Beast had taken its toll.

"He's injured," Elenna said, pointing to Arcta's calloused hand. A puckered red wound ran across his leathery palm. Blue-black liquid oozed from the cut.

"Evil magic," Aroha said.

Tom took the phoenix talon from his shield and held the smooth, curved talisman over Arcta's wound. The redness quickly faded, and the scab healed, leaving nothing but a faint silver scar.

Arcta let out a groan and began to stir. Tom, Elenna and Aroha leapt away, their weapons raised, as the mountain giant heaved himself up to sitting. He rubbed his huge eye with a hairy fist, then blinked groggily. Tom felt a rush of relief as he saw that Arcta's single brown eye had lost its reddish tinge, and he no longer looked angry – just tired and confused.

I'm sorry we struck you, Arcta, Tom told the Beast through his red jewel. *You were under an evil spell.*

Arcta rubbed his head, frowning, and spoke into Tom's mind in a low growl. *I remember…an old woman with a baby…lost. I showed them the way. But she cut me!* Arcta's gentle brown eye went wide. *I attacked you!*

Tom rested a hand on the mountain giant's huge arm. *It's all right. You were under a spell. My guess is Ospira used the power of her red stone to enslave you.*

She went that way! Arcta told Tom, pointing into the mountains. *I will bring her to you! She will pay...* Arcta lurched to his feet, but then staggered and slumped back to the ground, holding his head in both hands.

You are still weak from the magic, Tom told Arcta. *Too weak to face more witchcraft. But you can help us another way. Look for Aduro. Keep him safe if you can. We will find Ospira and baby Thomas.*

Tom turned to Elenna and the Queen. "Arcta says Ospira took Prince Thomas into the mountains. But I don't understand. If she can use her amulet to control any Beast she pleases, what does she want with Thomas?"

"It doesn't matter what she wants," the queen said fiercely. "She will not harm my son! Now let's go."

As they started to climb, the air before them swam like rising heat, and an image formed: a room in the palace; a desk with a book; and behind the desk, Daltec, looking grey with exhaustion.

The young wizard rested a hand on Ospira's open journal.

"I've been reading Ospira's last few entries," he said urgently. "I need to tell you what I've found."

Tom took a deep breath. *Something tells me this Quest is about to get tougher...*

OSPIRA'S JOURNAL:
EXILE

There's no turning back now! It is done! I have fled the palace!

I sneaked into my brother's room while he was off feasting with Hugo and Taladon. Maybe Harkman or some other slinking spy told him, but somehow he knew I was there. He caught me leaving his chamber with the red stone in my hand. Naturally,

I played dumb. I told him I was just borrowing it to go with an outfit. What does he want with jewellery anyhow?

But he wasn't fooled. He tried to snatch it from me, so I was forced to disable him. Nothing permanent, just a little freezing spell, though I suppose he'll be quite stiff for a few days. Ha! The look in his eyes was just priceless. I don't suppose he ever guessed I could wield such power! All the same, I wish I'd used a stronger spell, because somehow he managed to raise the alarm.

And who should my brother send after me but that prize pain in the neck, Taladon the Perfect, on his trusty steed.

Of course, that village idiot would

have been no trouble at all, except
that he sneaked up on me in my sleep.
I woke with a blade to my throat
and his oh-so-noble eyes gazing
sorrowfully into mine. Frankly, there
wasn't much I could do but listen
while he lectured me. On and on he

went about how I couldn't handle the power of Derthsin's stone. That I would become its tool and it would all end in woe and disaster.

He even had the nerve to say it was corrupting me already – as if being patronised and prevented from using my gifts by my own brother and his stupid friends wasn't enough reason to strike out on my own. Luckily, that gullible dupe of a so-called hero will fall for any old sob story. I told him I was sorry, squeezed out a few tears, and bam! He was eating out of my hand.

As soon as he put down his sword to comfort me, I froze him, just like I had frozen my brother. I wasn't taking any chances this time, so it

might take Taladon rather longer to defrost... Serves him right! If any of them had treated me with the respect I deserve, instead of like a foolish girl who should stick to needlework, none of this would have happened!

And now I'm off to find myself a nice quiet hiding place to experiment with my new toy. I will use it to succeed where even Derthsin feared to tread. I will create a Beast of my own, to do my bidding. Then my brother and Hugo and even Taladon will have to admit, I am no child to be scolded and ignored – I am Ospira, and my name will go down in history as the greatest sorceress of them all!

7

HORROR IN THE MIST

The image of Daltec with Ospira's
journal swirled and began to fade.
"Don't go!" Tom cried, a host of
questions burning inside him. But
it was too late. He let out a growl of
frustration as the vision disappeared.
"I wonder why my father never
mentioned any of this before," Tom
said. "It sounds like he knew Ospira

well enough back then."

"Probably out of loyalty to Aduro," Elenna said. "Aduro was the kingdom's wizard, after all – a position of great trust. If the people found out his sister was experimenting with Evil Magic and trying to create her own Beast, they might have lost faith in him too."

Aroha shuddered. "Let's waste no more time thinking about Aduro and that woman," she snapped. "My baby needs me." She struck off up the mountain.

Tom turned to Arcta, who, though standing now, still looked stooped and tired. *Farewell, friend,* he said. *Send word if you find Aduro. And please watch over Storm and*

*Hurricane until we return – we
cannot take them on the path we will
follow.* Arcta nodded, scooping up the
lead reins of the horses in his massive
fingers, then turned to lumber away.

Tom and Elenna set off after Aroha,

following a narrow, winding path upwards. The trail, little more than a crumbling ledge to begin with, soon petered out, leaving them to pick their way between sharp outcrops and gaping fissures. A cold wind wailed around them, tearing at Tom's hair and clothes. As he climbed, his boots slipped on ice and loose scree, making his heart leap into his mouth again and again.

Aroha turned suddenly, her hand raised. "Listen!" she hissed. Tom stopped and tilted his head. Along with the howl of the icy wind, he could just make out the thin, high wail of a baby. He turned his head, trying to locate the sound, but with the wind echoing off rocks all around them, it was impossible.

"Hurry!" Aroha cried, heading up the treacherous slope at an unsteady, lurching run. Tom and Elenna followed.

As the way grew steeper, Tom found himself using his hands as much as his feet, pulling himself up on ledges or wedging his fingers into cracks in the rock. His hands soon throbbed with pain and cold, but the prince's cries pulled him on, forcing him to ignore the pain in his muscles and the cuts to his skin. Aroha and Elenna climbed alongside him, grunting with effort, but never slowing their pace.

Eventually, when the air felt almost too thin to breathe, Tom heaved himself up on to a snow-covered

plateau. A crooked trail snaked downward towards a narrow valley cradled high in the mountain range. Dense fog hung over the valley, and though the sun still shone with a pale, white light, the swirling vapour had a sickly red tinge to it.

"That mist doesn't look natural," Elenna said. Suddenly, the loud wail of a baby reached them, much clearer than before, and definitely coming from the valley beneath them.

"Down there!" Aroha said. "Quickly!"

Tom, Elenna and Aroha scrambled down the rocky slope, half running, half sliding. Tendrils of red mist snaked around them, swirling in strange eddies, filling Tom's mouth and nose with the grave-like scent of mould and clay. His skin shrank from the vile, clammy touch of the mist, but he pressed on as fast as he could. Finally, the ground levelled. Aroha broke into a run, racing across the valley floor. Thick fog clouded Tom's vision as he followed, but soon he could just make out the shadowy shape of a bundle on the ground, lying before the gaping darkness of a cave mouth in the far valley wall. A pair of pink fists jabbed upwards from the bundle, pumping the air angrily in time with the prince's cries. Tom's every instinct screamed a warning. *This feels too easy...*

"Thomas!" Aroha gasped, leaping forward. Tom caught her arm and pulled her back.

"It's a trap!" he hissed. At the same moment, movement stirred in the darkness of the cave mouth. Tom's breath lodged in his throat as a giant, hunched figure unfolded from the gloom. The creature – some sort of Beastly woman – had bony limbs and skin like charred leather. Tom felt horror and revulsion rise from his gut. A filthy, ragged dress hung loose from the Beast's skeletal frame. Her bony face looked like little more than a skull, and dark red eyes like burning coals stared out from sunken sockets. Clasped in one gnarled, taloned fist, the Beast brandished a wooden staff, tipped with Ospira's glinting talisman.

"Let me go!" Aroha cried, straining against Tom's grip as the monstrous apparition stepped towards her baby, its thin lips pulled back to reveal curved teeth, dripping with saliva.

"Stay back!" Tom ordered the Beast-woman, a cold sweat breaking out on his skin. *Ospira! What evil have you done?*

STORY TWO

A FINAL SACRIFICE

In my younger days, when my magic was powerful, I could summon fire from my fingertips. I could use any number of spells to fill my belly with food. No more. I shiver in the cold, hunger gnawing at my insides. I am no wizard now. I am an old man, trying foolishly to make amends.

My destination is close. I feel it. I feel her nearby. My dear, troubled sister.

I fear what she has planned. With the curse infecting her blood, she is capable of terrible Evil.

Another freezing gust almost blows me over. Whatever was I thinking, coming here? Even if I find Ospira, what can I hope to do? I should never have come here alone. I should have told the king and queen of my fears. Only a true hero can put an end to this horror.

Aduro,
former wizard to King Hugo

1

OSPIRA'S BEAST

A sick terror burned inside Tom as
the skeletal monster leaned over
Prince Thomas, teeth bared. Queen
Aroha wrenched her arm from his
grip. "Get away from my baby!"
she roared, charging forwards,
brandishing her sword. The Beast-
woman looked up, her red eyes
narrowing as they fixed on the queen.
Tom leapt after Aroha, sword raised.

But before he could reach her, the Beast let out a hiss of rage and swung her staff with inhuman speed, slamming it into Aroha's body. The queen flew through the air, landing hard on her side. Her head cracked against a rock and she lay still.

"Aroha!" Elenna cried, rushing towards her.

Panic struck Tom's heart. *Is she dead?*

The Beast leaned over the baby once more, but Tom leapt forwards, sending his blade whistling down. *CLANG!* The woman blocked his swipe with her staff. Tom almost dropped his sword, arm ringing with pain from the impact. *She's so strong!* The Beast moved again in a ragged blur of speed, her staff lashing down. Tom threw up his shield.

BOOF! He gasped and staggered back, reeling with agony from the blow.

Whoosh! An arrow whistled past Tom. It struck the Beast's shoulder and lodged there. The creature growled and glanced about. As her smouldering eyes fell on Elenna, she gave a hissing laugh. Then she plucked the arrow from her shoulder and tossed it aside. No blood flowed from the wound – just a trickle of dust. Tom swallowed. *What kind of a monster has Ospira created?*

Elenna let a second arrow fly. *THUD!* It slammed into the Beast-woman's chest. With a furious growl, the hideous creature dived towards Elenna and Aroha.

Ignoring the pain in his arms, Tom lunged for the screaming prince. But before he could reach the blanketed bundle, he heard a sizzling fizz. Elenna let out a yelp. Tom turned to see her leap away from the queen, then throw herself down on the ground, flames licking at her tunic. The Beast cackled with laughter, the red tip of her staff pointed at Elenna.

As Elenna rolled, a jet of red energy shot from the tip of the Beast's staff and struck the ground beside her, turning it to a roiling puddle of molten rock. Elenna scrambled away, clutching one arm to her chest. Tom could see a raw burn where her sleeve had been singed away.

Aroha groaned suddenly, and began to stir. The Beast-woman let out a dry, breathy cackle, then pointed the fiery tip of her staff at the queen.

No! Tom called on the power of his golden boots and leapt, soaring over the Beast's head. He landed in a crouch at Aroha's side and threw up his shield. A glowing energy beam shot from the tip of the Beast's staff towards him. Tom angled his shield,

hoping to deflect the beam with
Ferno's dragon scale. As the fire struck,
Tom felt a blast of heat so intense it
seemed to sear the inside of his throat.
He braced his arms, holding his shield

steady. Sweat streamed down his face. He struggled to breathe, his throat closing against scorching flames pouring around the wood.

Behind him, Aroha groaned once more and tried to move. "Stay down!" Tom growled, his voice little more than a croak. His arms shook, and his head throbbed. He could feel his belt buckle and the metal buttons of his tunic blistering his skin through his clothes. Suddenly, just as Tom's vision started to blur and he thought he might pass out, the Beast gave a harsh bark of laughter, and the searing heat stopped. Tom slumped down on his hands and knees, gasping for breath. With nightmarish speed, the Beast hobbled to the prince's side.

"NO!" Aroha cried weakly, as the vile creature leaned over her baby and reached out her taloned hands.

Tom watched in helpless horror, too sick and dizzy to move. *Don't hurt him!* But the hunched monster simply snatched up the child, then turned and lurched away towards the cave mouth with her swift, unsteady stride.

"Stop!" Tom bellowed. "I will fight you for the child. One on one…a fair duel." As he spoke he touched the red jewel as well. Even if the Beast's hearing was poor, the magic would drive his message into her brain.

Sure enough, the Beast turned to gaze back over her shoulder, her hollow eyes suddenly turning as cold and dark as the abyss. She let out a

grating laugh. *This is my child*, her voice rasped in Tom's mind. *Anyone who tries to take him will die.* Then she turned and plunged into the darkness of the cave, and was gone.

OSPIRA'S JOURNAL:
THE HAND OF EVIL

Back at the palace, Daltec leaned close to the diary entry before him, straining his eyes to read Ospira's looping script in the dying light from his fire. He knew he should light a candle, but he couldn't bring himself to stop reading. A loud rap on the door made him jump. He looked up to see his study door swing open. King Hugo stepped through, dressed in a riding cloak over full armour which glinted in the firelight.

"I can't stay here a moment longer!" Hugo said. "I must go after them!"

Daltec put up a hand. "Your Majesty, I know my words will be unwelcome, but the kingdom needs a ruler. Tom and Elenna will not fail you. They will bring your son back. Your place is here, at the palace."

King Hugo rubbed his face with both hands. Then he let out a frustrated growl. "You are right," he told Daltec. "Of course, you are right. But my heart feels as if it will burn a hole in my chest." The king's eyes fell on the journal laid before Daltec. "Tell me," he said, "have you learned anything more about Ospira?"

Daltec nodded, suddenly filled with dread. "I have," he said, then turned back a few yellowed pages, and started to read:

My hand is unsteady because I write these words in near darkness and in much pain. I am unsure even now if I am closer to victory or to destruction. But one thing I do know is that some new power burns inside me, and I will wield it if I can.

I travelled far in search of a suitable place for my research, deep into the Northern Mountains. Finally, I came upon a sheltered valley. I lit a fire and made my camp safe in the knowledge that I would not be disturbed.

Unfortunately, even this didn't stop my brother interfering with my plans.

I had spoken the sacred words, and cast the runes of Derthsin. I had sprinkled rare and powerful herbs upon my fire and breathed their smoke. Then, as I prepared to utter the final incantation, Aduro appeared.

I soon realised I was looking at nothing but an apparition – a projection of Aduro's form, with his body still back at the palace. I could even see the walls of my brother's study flickering behind him. I told him to leave me – that I was finally about to realise my full potential. But instead he pleaded with me, wasting precious time. He begged me to stop, claiming that I would release untold horrors from Derthsin's stone. He told me it was not too late to return to the palace – that Hugo would forgive me, and that even Taladon, once he had recovered, would be sure to accept my apology.

Ha! To seek forgiveness from that conceited buffoon! Even the thought sickens me.

"I don't want anything from you or your friends!" I told my brother. Then I summoned a magical wind and blasted Aduro's image to shreds. Even as my brother's pathetic spell failed, he continued to plead with me, telling me he could not protect me if I chose the path of Evil. Well, I don't need his protection, and I never have. I told him

as much. Maybe my words reached him, for he spoke no more, and did not return.

With my brother gone, I resumed my work. I thrust the magical stone of Derthsin right into the heart of the fire, just as the Chronicles of Avantia *had instructed. The stone began to glow so brightly, its sharp afterimage is still etched into my brain.*

But something went wrong. I shudder even as I write of it. As the stone glowed ever brighter, a sinewy red arm reached from the flames and snatched my wrist. Though I pulled with all my strength, the monstrous arm tugged my hand over the heart of the fire.

The pain was like nothing I have felt before. I screamed and struggled,

but the demonic hand held my palm
mercilessly over the flames until I
could smell the singeing of my own
flesh. I heard a hideous cackle, and

finally, I was able to pull my hand free. I fled into a cave and cradled my injured arm. I have bathed it now, and bandaged it with a healing poultice. But despite this, and though my fire is long out, my injured flesh yet burns as if still held above the flames.

But there is something else, something that gives me hope and scares me at the same time. Since attempting the spell, I have felt strangely different – in a way I can't describe.

But one thing I am sure of: just as the fire touched my hand, burning my flesh, I heard a voice. A voice that spoke in a vile, hissing buzz. It said four words: "The Beast is coming!"

Daltec laid the journal on the desk before him and looked up to see cold horror etched into the lines of King Hugo's face.

"Ospira unleashed some dark evil," Hugo said. "Tom and Elenna…Aroha… they are all heading into terrible danger."

Daltec took a deep breath, seeking to show the king a calm he did not feel. "Tom and Elenna face Evil on every Quest," Daltec said. "The queen, when roused to anger, is a force both terrible and just. If there is a way to bring Prince Thomas home, they will find it."

The king took a few paces, wringing his hands, then turned to Daltec. "I can only pray you are right," he said. As Hugo left the room, Daltec slumped

back in his chair, all the worry and
horror he'd been hiding from the king
washing over him in a tide. *I can only
hope so too.*

3

VARKULE ATTACK

Tom stared towards the cave mouth after the Beast, and the prince's cries echoed in his mind. *I have to help baby Thomas!* Ignoring the surge of dizziness that gripped him, Tom started to push himself up. He felt a weak tug on his tunic and glanced back to see Queen Aroha propped up on one arm, swaying.

"Go!" Aroha croaked, before

sinking back to the ground. Nearby, Elenna was struggling up. Her clothes still smoked, but her eyes shone with a fierce light.

"Let's hurry!" she said.

Tom nodded. "We won't return until we have the prince," he promised the queen, then he and Elenna strode towards the cave mouth.

Only a few paces inside the cave, the ground sloped sharply downwards. The light filtering through the entrance faded, leaving them in inky darkness. From somewhere deep inside the mountain, Tom could hear baby Thomas crying.

"Stay close," Tom told Elenna. He reached out a hand to trace the tunnel wall and started to shuffle

downwards, his eyes straining to see
in the dark. Mingled with the prince's
distant cries, Tom could hear the

sound of water trickling. The deeper
the path led them, the louder the
sound of running water became, until
a rushing roar echoed all around. A
soft orange glow appeared ahead.

The light grew steadily brighter
as they hurried onwards, until the
tunnel walls glittered with seams of
shining quartz and Tom could make
out slender stalactites hanging from
the ceiling.

As they rounded the bend, the
tunnel ended abruptly. Light spilled
from a curved archway before them.
Prince Thomas's whimpers echoed
through the arch, along with the
swoosh of flowing water.

Tom tightened his grip on his sword
and took a deep breath. Elenna

lifted her bow and they both stepped through the entrance. A vast chamber opened around them, the curved walls marked with ridges as if carved by sharp tools. Smoking torches set in sconces made the shadows bob and dance.

About a dozen huge, irregular stones, so big even Arcta would struggle to lift them, stood at intervals around the chamber wall. Through a stalactite-fringed opening at the back, Tom could see the glimmer of an underground river flowing into darkness. Poised on the riverbank, framed by the tooth-like stalactites, stood the Beast. She clutched baby Thomas in one arm, holding him tightly to her sunken chest. In her other hand, she held the stone-tipped staff. She beckoned Tom and Elenna with it, her eyes glowing with deep red light.

"Give me the child!" Tom shouted. The Beast extended the staff, and he raised his shield. But the red beam that shot forth from the shard of stone split off in several directions. They each fell across the standing stones and plumes of smoke rose as the rock began to melt, glowing red hot. The Beast let out a hollow cackle and, turning, disappeared further into darkness. Tom had just set off in pursuit when Elenna caught his arm.

"Look!" she cried, pointing to the nearest standing stone. In the half-light, Tom saw jagged cracks

zigzagging up the stone as it cooled
from red to orange. Chunks of rock
fell away, clattering to the ground to
reveal something *living* underneath.
Something with dark, mangy fur
and bulging muscles. As more stone

crumbled loose, Tom saw toothy jaws with jutting tusks and recognised the creature at once. *A Varkule!* Tom clenched his teeth, frustration filling his chest. The terrifying giant hyena had been extinct in Avantia for over a century, yet somehow this pack had been preserved in the enchanted columns of rock. *We don't have time for this!*

The first Varkule to free itself shook its fur wildly, showering Tom with chips of stone. It gave a deep, echoing growl, which was quickly answered by the others as they emerged from their rocky coffins.

"Tom," Elenna whispered, "we're surrounded." Glancing about, Tom could see at least twelve pairs of hungry eyes reflecting the torchlight, and twelve sets of snarling yellow teeth. Where the standing stones had been, rubble littered the cavern floor.

Tom sank into a crouch, poised lightly on the balls of his feet, ready to strike. At his side, Elenna notched an arrow to her bow and took aim. As the Varkules padded slowly closer, Tom glanced between them, trying to gauge which would pounce first. Suddenly, two monsters leapt at once, one from either side of him, letting out fierce growls.

Tom jumped back, tugging Elenna with him. *BOOF!* The Varkules slammed together headfirst, then slumped to the ground, shaking their muzzles. Tom lunged, plunging his

blade deep into the hairy flank of
the nearest. Elenna sent her arrow
thudding into the hide of the other. As
Tom withdrew his blade, the tufty fur
and sinewy flesh before him hardened
to grey stone, then crumbled in an

instant, leaving a pile of rubble. Elenna's target crumbled too, but more creatures advanced steadily towards them from every side.

A hideous snarl echoed from behind Tom. He spun to see a mass of muscle and teeth hurtling his way.

"No, you don't!" Elenna cried, firing. *Swoosh!* Her arrow sank deep into the monster's side. Its eyes widened as it hardened to rock in midair, then broke apart in a hail of rubble. Tom threw up his shield to protect them both. The shattered remains of the creature pelted down, rattling against the wood.

Three more Varkules pounced. Adrenaline jolted through Tom's veins, sharpening his senses, lending him speed. Curved claws, hungry eyes and snarling muzzles barrelled towards him, but Tom focussed on the Varkules' exposed underbellies. His sword whistled through the air, slicing and jabbing. A pair of curved tusks stabbed his way. Tom swung his shield, slamming them aside, then thrust his sword into the Varkule's broad chest. Elenna's bow sang as she fired arrow after arrow.

With every killing blow, chips of stone cascaded down, scattering across the floor. Tom's boots crunched on the remains of his fallen enemies, but still they came. Hot breath rasped in his throat and his arms ached as he slashed and thrusted.

On the far side of the cave, Tom

spotted two Varkules charging towards Elenna at once. She held her ground, one eye narrowed as she gazed along her bow, two arrows fitted to the string. Elenna fired. *Thud! Thunk!* Both creatures fell, turning into a clattering shower of pebbles as they hit the cave floor, but yet another creature was rushing towards her.

"Watch out!" Tom cried, shoving his sword into a Varkule's stinking pelt. Elenna turned, but too late. The creature cannoned into her, throwing her to the floor and knocking her bow from her hand. *NO!* Tom dived towards his friend, but more Varkules blocked his path. He gritted his teeth and stabbed the nearest through the

throat, then slammed his shield hard
into another's thick skull. Torchlight
flickered in Elenna's eyes, wide with
fear, as she skittered backwards away
from the Varkule bearing down on
her. But with the river right behind

her, Tom could see she was trapped.

Calling on the power of his golden boots, Tom leapt towards the snapping brute advancing on his friend, angling his sword downwards in midair. As Tom landed, his blade bit deep into reeking flesh, skewering the Varkule right through. As it disintegrated, Elenna sagged with relief, then scrambled to her feet.

"What now?" she hissed, her face pale in the half-dark as she surveyed the cavern. Five huge creatures remained, each glaring their way, hackles raised and saliva dripping from their tusks. A dark hole gaped behind Tom and Elenna, and Tom could feel the cold chill of a breeze on his skin. He heard the thunder of water rushing by.

Tom craned his neck to peer through the opening. The underground river had carved a tunnel in the rock. On one side, a narrow ledge led downwards beside the river, in the same direction the water flowed. On the other side, the dark current lapped right up against the tunnel walls with no bank at all.

"The Beast must have gone deeper into the caves," Tom said, "the same way the river flows. The current is fast. Maybe we'll catch up with her if we swim." Eyeing the Varkules steadily closing in on them, Elenna nodded. "It's worth a try," she said. She hooked her bow over her shoulders, then, with one last look back into the cavern, she turned and leapt into the torrent. In an instant, the dark water swept Elenna away. Tom sheathed his sword, took a deep breath and jumped in after her.

Icy fingers seemed to close around

him, squeezing the air from his chest
and snatching him into swirling
darkness. He pumped his arms
and legs, trying to stay afloat, but
a powerful current dragged him
under. Freezing water filled his eyes

and nose. He spun and swirled, sucked onwards and downwards by the torrent speeding around him. His shoulder slammed into a rock, then his head, making him draw a mouthful of water. His throat and lungs burned and panic gripped hold of him... *This was a terrible mistake! We're going to drown!*

THE HEART OF
THE MOUNTAIN

Just as Tom thought his lungs would
burst if he didn't breathe, he felt
himself sucked downwards. Suddenly,
he was falling through air, gasping
as water pelted down all around
him. *SPLASH!* He landed in more
freezing water and plunged down
through red-tinged darkness. He
kicked his legs, swimming up, his

lungs screaming for more air. Finally, he broke through the surface and gasped, drawing in great breaths.

Relief surged through him as he spotted Elenna spluttering and gasping nearby, her hair plastered to her head as she trod water to stay afloat. They had arrived in a cavern. The whole place was suffused with an unnatural red light which turned the waterfall and pool around Tom a bloody shade. Beyond the water's edge Tom could see baby Thomas, whimpering softly, lying on a slab of stone that reminded him of a simple altar. Behind the baby stood the Beast-woman, her staff raised and her eyes lit with triumphant glee as she chanted harsh, guttural words in

a strange tongue.

"Stop!" Tom cried, first swimming, then wading from the pool with Elenna at his side. The Beast barely glanced at Tom and Elenna before returning her intense gaze to the baby. The whole cavern flickered with hellish light as the tip of the Beast's staff glowed red. Strands of bright energy, like forked lightning, cracked from the glowing stone and sizzled downwards towards Prince Thomas. As the forked strands touched down, the baby's cries stopped abruptly. He froze, surrounded by searing red light.

"What is she doing? We have to stop her!" Elenna cried, drawing an arrow from her quiver. Then she glanced at a nearby torch. "I think I'll give her a taste of her own medicine," she said.

Elenna tore a strip of fabric from her sleeve and wrapped it tightly around the tip of her arrow. Then she snatched the torch from a sconce on the wall and held the arrow tip to the flame.

The soaked fabric spluttered and

sizzled, but didn't light.

"It's too wet!" Elenna exclaimed.

"Let me try," said Tom. He took the torch from her, drew back his arm and flung it with all his strength. The flames left a trail of smoke as the torch spun through the air, before striking the hem of the Beast's tattered robe. *Whoosh!* Hungry flames crackled up the dry cloth. The Beast gasped and dropped her staff, her red eyes wide with panic. She threw herself down and began to roll, frantically, over and over, as the flames engulfed her form.

Prince Thomas started to wail once more. Red streams of energy sizzled from the tip of the Beast's fallen staff, crackling around the prince, still somehow connected to him. Tom crossed to the altar and swept his sword through the magical strands, severing them. The red light surrounding baby Thomas flickered and went out. Elenna snatched the howling child from the stone slab and cradled him closely. As the prince's panicked cries softened, Tom stormed towards the Beast-woman, rage burning in his chest. She lay still, the flames that had engulfed her finally dying. Her charred clothing smoked on her wizened frame. Tom couldn't see her chest rising and falling, but he had to be sure. He leaned in closer. Hissing, the Beast snatched at his leg with scorched hands. Tom wrenched his foot away, then raised his sword to

deliver a mortal blow.

"No!" cried an old, familiar voice.
Tom turned to see the hunched
figure of Aduro hurrying from a side
passage, one hand raised. "Please,
stop!" the old man cried, throwing

himself between Tom and the Beast.
"Please don't harm her."

Tom gaped, his sword still raised
as he stared at his old friend. A
ragged gasp of breath from the Beast
brought Tom back to his senses.
"Aduro, move out of the way," he
ordered the former wizard. "Your

sister brought Prince Thomas here, as some sort of gift for this Evil Beast. I have to put an end to it!"

Aduro shook his head, his eyes filled with terror and sorrow. "You don't understand!" the former wizard sobbed. "This Beast *is* my sister." He gestured to the burned form on the ground. "This is Ospira."

OSPIRA'S JOURNAL:
TO THE BITTER END

Daltec read on by flickering candlelight, his nose almost touching the paper as he struggled to make out Ospira's untidy red scrawl. Each new word he managed to decipher struck a new chord of horror inside him, and a terrible sadness clutched at his heart as he finally began to understand...

*Aduro, my dear brother, I hope you
find these words after I am gone,
and though I know I cannot expect
forgiveness, at least you will have the
truth. I am so sorry. No one is to blame
but myself, I see that now. I have made*

a terrible mistake.

Something horrible went wrong when I used the amulet of Derthsin, just as you said it would. I was a fool to ever think I could control its power. For days after casting the *spell, I suffered from headaches so painful I wanted to bash in my own brains. At first, I couldn't admit to myself that I was changing, though my bones ached, and I itched all over. But before long, my hair began to fall out in clumps. And then my teeth. As I look at my arm, I can see the dry skin hanging slack on my bones as the flesh wastes away. And yet I am strong enough to break rocks with my fists. I am taller too.*

I am transforming into something different. Something horrible. I caught a glimpse of myself when drinking from a still mountain pool, and the sight of my own face filled me with terror. It was not only my altered form and pale, wizened skin, but the terrible

cruelty I saw in my eyes...

Aduro, I was trying to summon a Beast – but somehow, I think, I have become one. A dark spirit lurks inside me, and it grows stronger with each day. It tells me to do terrible things – to use the shard to create a new race of Beast-human hybrids like myself. But I won't do that to Avantia. I can feel my will failing – my very self being crushed to nothing inside my soul. But I think I have found a solution. While I still can, I will travel deep into the network of caves that run beneath the mountains. Then I will use magic to cause a landslide, collapsing the entrance behind me, trapping myself inside. There, whatever I become, I can do no harm.

I write this last entry using the blood of a mountain lion I killed with my own hands, but I can't write much longer. I can barely hold the quill, it is so tiny in my monstrous fingers.

I must act quickly before it is too late.

Aduro, please believe me, I only ever wanted to be respected, and to be remembered – to have other people see my worth – but now the whole world must forget I existed. The name of Ospira must fade through the ages and forever be erased.

I hear two voices inside my mind now, and I hardly know which is my own!

One voice tells me I am just the first of my kind – a creature powerful beyond measure. Using the amulet of Derthsin I can create others just like me!

No! I will not. I cannot let the Beast take over. As long as there is human blood in my veins, I will fight this evil to the bitter end. But Aduro, my dear brother, I know I cannot win...

A NEW BEAST
AWAKES

Aduro sat beside the smouldering, now lifeless remains of his sister, and wiped his eyes with the hem of his cloak even as new sobs racked his body.

Tom put a hand on the old man's shoulder. Having listened as Aduro recounted Ospira's tale, he knew how much pain his friend must feel.

"If only I had listened to her…" Aduro said. "She just wanted to learn, but the kingdom was in peril. We were all so wrapped up in our own concerns, and she was so very young…

"When I found her journal in the mountains, I vowed to save her. I studied every book I could get my hands on, but I never found a spell to lift Derthsin's curse. So instead, I created an enchanted mist here in the mountains to keep everyone away. It tore me apart. I never told anyone. Not Taladon, not Hugo." Aduro let out another shuddering sob. "Oh, Ospira, please forgive me!"

"You did what you could," Elenna said, pacing the cave floor, joggling

baby Thomas in her arms. "You
couldn't do more."

Aduro shook his head sorrowfully.
"When I heard of earthquakes in this
region, I returned here to make sure
my sister was still trapped."

"You had no choice," Tom said. "But in the end, you were too late. She had already escaped and used magic to return to Avantia in her human form. I suppose she was planning to create more Beasts like herself."

Aduro nodded, his eyes on the fallen body of his sister. Tom saw a look of horror cross the old man's face. He followed Aduro's gaze to see a shudder run through Ospira's charred form. Suddenly, a strange red light surrounded her. The light rose up, peeling away from the lifeless body in a ghostly likeness of the Beast.

Aduro let out a yelp of fear and shot to his feet.

"What's happening?" Elenna cried. Tom lifted his sword and lunged,

but the ghost-Beast leapt away from him, slamming straight into Aduro, throwing the old man to the floor. It swept right over Aduro's body and sped towards Elenna and the prince.

"No!" Tom yelled, bending his knees and using the power of his golden boots to leap high into the air. He landed before Elenna and spun, his sword raised. The ghostly form of the Beast, now more shrivelled and hideous than ever, opened her mouth and hissed, her face contorted with rage.

Tom held his ground. "If you want the child," he cried, "you'll have to fight me for him!"

I think not! the Beast said, speaking into Tom's mind in a breathy rasp that made his skin crawl. Her eyes glowed suddenly as bright as two suns and, with impossible speed and strength, she thrust a hand forwards, right inside Tom's chest. He froze, his breath catching in his throat, his whole body stiff with agony as evil fingers closed powerfully around his

heart and squeezed.

Yes… the Beast's rasping, evil voice hissed in his mind. *This body will be a worthy vehicle for my spirit.* The red apparition pulsed with light as hot waves of energy flowed into Tom, filling him with blood-boiling, murderous rage. Tom gasped. His chest felt like it might burst with the fury building inside him. He let out a roar and tightened his grip on his sword as more and more Evil energy flooded his soul. A part of him, trapped deep inside, quaked in fear.

I'm becoming a Beast, just like Ospira!

NEVER FORGOTTEN

A red haze seemed to surround Tom. His head throbbed, and his chest burned with a desperate need to destroy, to shed blood. With one hand still buried deep in Tom's chest, the ghost-Beast lifted her head, grinning wildly, as if drinking in the joy of her victory.

Suddenly, through the red mist that

clouded his vision, Tom saw a blazing white form approaching, pure and terrible, filled with light. *Aroha!* Tom realised, just as the queen lifted her sword and brought it down with a *snick!* The blade severed the Beast's

ghostly wrist and Tom felt the grip on his heart release. At once, the boiling fury inside him evaporated.

He slumped to his knees, gasping, the red mist gone. He glanced up to see the Beast turned into a simple woman again, but one whose eyes sparkled with fury. Ospira turned on the queen with a hiss, swiping for her with curved talons. Aroha brought her sword down once more, lopping off the monster's other hand.

"That's for taking my baby!" she growled. The Beast let out a furious roar and reached for the queen again, two grisly stumps where her hands had been. To Tom's horror, new hands grew with awful speed, and groped for Aroha's throat. The queen gasped and stepped back. Her foot caught on a rock, and she fell, the sword spinning from her hand. With a hiss of triumph, the Beast surged forwards and lifted a huge foot above Aroha, ready to stomp on her chest. The queen rolled away.

"Tom! Use the staff!" Aduro cried. "The shard summoned the Beast. The shard must be the key to defeating it!" At Aduro's words, the Beast turned away from the queen, her hollow eyes suddenly fearful. Her huge staff lay where it had fallen, beside the altar. The Beast lunged towards it. *No!* Summoning every last shred of strength remaining to him, Tom shot to his feet. He bent double and careered forwards, half running, half stumbling, his eyes on the glowing red shard.

His hand closed on knobbly wood. He tried to lift the giant staff, but it felt as heavy as iron. He glanced back to see the Beast right behind him, jaws wide open in a furious rictus of hate. Tom dropped his sword and, calling on the magical strength of his breastplate, hefted up the staff in both hands and turned it on the Evil spirit.

The red apparition's expression changed from hate to a grimace of fear. Moving too fast to stop, the Beast lurched on, falling right on to the tip of the staff, impaling herself though the stomach. The monstrous creature froze, her eyes and mouth opened wide in shock. For an instant, a strange silence filled the cave, as if

even the flowing water had stopped in
its path. Tom tugged the staff from the
Beast's body to see the red tip glowing
fiercely. The Beast's form began to

swirl and eddy, then in less than a heartbeat it flowed right into the glowing stone as if sucked away by a strong current.

All at once, the noise returned to the cave. Tom could hear Aroha weeping with joy as she cradled her son. He could hear Aduro weeping too: painful-sounding, dry sobs. He turned to see the old man cradling a young woman with long black curls and a deathly pale face.

Tom and Elenna hurried to Aduro's side. "Ospira!" Tom said. The woman's eyes fluttered open. They were clear and grey and filled with gratitude.

"Thank you, Tom," she croaked, her voice barely more than a whisper. "I never thought it would be Taladon's son who freed me! Your father would have been proud." She smiled faintly, and her eyes flickered closed for a moment. When they opened again, they gazed up into Aduro's face. "Can you ever forgive me, brother?" Ospira asked.

"Of course!" Aduro said, his cracked voice thick with tears. "And I promise, your story will live on. I will make sure your name is never forgotten."

Tom turned away for a few moments, to give Aduro and his sister some privacy in her final breaths. When he looked back again, Ospira's eyes were closed and the former wizard was weeping quietly.

A warm sun shone over the palace gardens as Tom laid a wreath of yellow and purple flowers on the mound of earth before him. Fresh blooms already covered more than half the grave. He stepped back to stand with Elenna, alongside King Hugo and Aduro.

"This is a lovely spot, Your Majesty," Aduro said, smiling. His eyes were still raw from tears.

"I thought she would like to be laid to rest here," Hugo said. "She deserves a proper memorial, after everything she went through. She might have made some poor choices, but in the end, she sacrificed herself to protect us all from great Evil." Hugo turned to Tom. "Which reminds me, what will you do with the shard? We cannot allow such powerful Evil to fall into the wrong hands again."

Tom heard the whoosh of giant wingbeats, and smiled. "I have already thought of that!" he said. A moment later, Epos, gleaming with glossy red and gold plumage, landed with a thump beside them. The Good Beast cocked her massive head, watching Tom with her amber eyes. Tom unclipped the golden chain from around his neck, and held the red amulet out to the flame bird.

Epos opened her huge beak to receive the red stone.

"Take this to Stonewin's crater," Tom told her. "There it will be melted down to nothing in the

furnace of the volcano."

Epos dipped her magnificent head,
then opened her wings and took
flight, soaring high into the clear

blue sky. When the great phoenix had dwindled to nothing more than a golden dot on the horizon, King Hugo turned to Tom and Elenna. "The kingdom is safe once more," Hugo said. "And we have you two to thank. But unfortunately, I can offer you no rest at the moment. I have a very important Quest for the pair of you."

Tom felt a jolt of alarm. *What threat does the kingdom face now?* He'd never felt so tired in his life, but he forced himself to look eager as he met the king's gaze. "Whatever you need from us, we are ready," he told the king. But then he noticed a familiar twinkle in Hugo's eye. Tom could see the monarch trying to stifle a smile.

"A cherry pie!" Tom and Elenna

said together. Tom laughed as relief washed through him. He knew that Evil would always be lurking, and he would always be ready to take it on. But that didn't mean he couldn't do with a break now and then…

THE END

CONGRATULATIONS,
YOU HAVE COMPLETED THIS QUEST!

At the end of each chapter you were awarded a special gold coin.
The QUEST in this book was worth an amazing 14 coins.

Look at the Beast Quest totem picture opposite to see how far you've come in your journey to become

MASTER OF THE BEASTS.

The more books you read, the more coins you will collect!

Do you want your own
Beast Quest Totem?

1. Cut out and collect the coin below
2. Go to the Beast Quest website
3. Download and print out your totem
4. Add your coin to the totem

www.beastquest.co.uk

READ THE BOOKS, COLLECT THE COINS!
EARN COINS FOR EVERY CHAPTER YOU READ!

550+ COINS
MASTER OF
THE BEASTS

410 COINS
HERO

350 COINS
WARRIOR

230 COINS
KNIGHT

180 COINS
SQUIRE

44 COINS
PAGE

8 COINS
APPRENTICE

*Look out for
the next series
of Beast Quest!
Read on for a
sneak peek at
QUERZOL
THE SWAMP
MONSTER...*

THE QUEEN'S BIRTHDAY

Music filled the courtyard and
dancing couples flitted past Tom as he
pushed his dinner plate away. "I can't
eat another bite," he sighed, turning
to Elenna, who sat beside him at the
banqueting table.

His friend put down the chicken

leg she'd been nibbling. "I guess that means two slices of Aroha's birthday cake for me, then," she said, smiling. Tom glanced up the table that ran the length of the courtyard, to where King Hugo and Queen Aroha sat on a raised dais. The jewels in the king's crown glinted as he nodded in time with the music. Beside him, the queen beamed as she watched the dancing couples. Nearby sat an enormous cake, baked in the shape of the queen's palace in Tangala, in honour of her birthday. Despite his full stomach Tom's mouth watered.

"Don't even think of taking my slice!" he said.

Read QUERZOL THE SWAMP MONSTER to find out more!